MR. GRUMPY

by Roger Hargreaves

It was a lovely summer evening.

Mr Grumpy was at home.

Crosspatch Cottage!

He sat down in an armchair, and picked up a book.

And then, do you know what he did?

He tore all the pages out of it!

Every one!

Mr Grumpy can't stand books.

He has a shocking bad temper.

In fact, he's quite the most bad-tempered person you can imagine.

Grumpy by name, and even more grumpy by nature!

The following morning, he was out in his garden pulling up flowers (he couldn't stand pretty flowers growing in his garden), when out of the corner of his eye he saw a figure.

It was Mr Happy.

"Good morning," said Mr Happy.

"Good?" said Mr Grumpy. "What's good about it?"

"But . . .," said Mr Happy.

"But nothing," went on Mr Grumpy. "Get out of my garden!"

"I beg your pardon?" said Mr Happy.

"You heard me," snapped Mr Grumpy. "Go away!"

"I say," laughed Mr Happy. "You are a bad-tempered fellow!"

"Hmph!" grunted Mr Grumpy.

"And," went on Mr Happy, "bad-tempered fellows need to change their ways."

"Rubbish!" retorted Mr Grumpy and went into his cottage, deliberately stepping on Mr Happy's foot as he passed him.

"Ouch!" said Mr Happy.

BANG! went the door of Crosspatch Cottage as Mr Grumpy slammed it behind him.

Mr Happy stood there, looking not quite so happy as he normally does.

His foot hurt!

He thought.

And thought.

And thought some more.

Then, he had an idea.

He smiled, and went to see Mr Tickle.

Mr Happy told Mr Tickle of his idea of how to get Mr Grumpy to change his ways, and Mr Tickle grinned the sort of grin that goes from ear to ear.

That is, if you have ears, which he doesn't.

"Oh," he grinned, rubbing the hands at the end of those extraordinarily long arms of his together. "That sounds fun!"

That afternoon, Mr Grumpy went to town, shopping.

He walked into Mr Meat's shop.

Mr Meat was a butcher.

"Give me some sausages," snapped Mr Grumpy. "And be quick about it!"

Poor Mr Meat, who was frightened of Mr Grumpy, did as he was told.

But, as he was doing as he was told, something appeared through his shop doorway.

Do you know what it was?

It was an extraordinarily long arm belonging to . . .

Well, you can guess who it belonged to.

Can't you?

That extraordinarily long arm of Mr Tickle's came in through the door, and across the shop, and up to Mr Grumpy, and tickled him.

"Oh!" squeaked Mr Grumpy in alarm, dropping his sausages, and looking round to see what had happened.

But, could he see anything?

He could not!

"Hmph!" grunted Mr Grumpy, and picked up his sausages, and went next door.

To the cake shop.

CRASH! went the door of the shop.

"Give me a cake," snapped Mr Grumpy. "And hurry up!"

Poor Mrs Fairy, who sold cakes, was frightened of Mr Grumpy, so did as she was told.

But, as she was doing as she was told, guess what happened?

"Oh!" squeaked Mr Grumpy, dropping his cake, and his sausages.

He just could not understand what was happening.

And, the same thing happened at Mr Daily's (the newspaper shop), and at Mrs Humbug's (the sweetshop), and at Mr Bottle's dairy, and at Mr Packet's (the grocer's).

It went on all afternoon!

And all afternoon Mr Grumpy kept being tickled,
and dropping his shopping, and picking it up, and
being tickled, and dropping his shopping, and
picking it up, and being tickled, and dropping his
shopping, and . . .

He just could not understand it.

On his way home to Crosspatch Cottage, he met Mr Happy again.

"Hello," grinned Mr Happy. "Having a nice day?"

"Get out of my way," snapped Mr Grumpy, "before I kick you!"

But, almost before the words had passed his lips, that extraordinarily long arm of Mr Tickle's had appeared from behind a tree and tickled him yet again.

He jumped in the air, and dropped all his shopping (yet again), and fell over.

Mr Happy looked down at Mr Grumpy lying amid a jumble of sausages and cake and newspapers and sweets and milk and cornflakes.

"I think," he laughed, "that if you were to change your ways and be not quite so bad-tempered quite so often, this sort of thing might not happen to you quite so often."

"Hmph!" grunted Mr Grumpy.

He picked up all his shopping (yet again) and went home to Crosspatch Cottage.

But on his way he did think about what Mr Happy had said, because he very definitely did not like what had happened to him that afternoon.

Mr Happy and Mr Tickle laughed and shook hands.

And so, after that, he did try to be not quite so bad-tempered quite so often.

And, the more he tried the less he found he was tickled, and so he tried more and more, and these days he's quite a changed person.

Why, only the other evening, he picked up a book, and do you know what?

He only tore out one page!

Fantastic offers for Mr. Men fans!

Collect all your Mr. Men or Little Miss books in these superb durable collectors' cases!
Only £5.99 inc. postage and packing, these wipe-clean, hard-wearing cases will give all your Mr. Men or Little Miss books a beautiful new home!

Keep track of your collection with this giant-sized double-sided Mr. Men and Little Miss Collectors' poster.
Collect 6 tokens and we will send you a brilliant giant-sized double-sided collectors' poster! Simply tape a £1 coin to cover postage and packaging in the space provided and fill out the form overleaf.

STICK £1 COIN HERE (for poster only)

Only need a few Mr. Men or Little Miss to complete your set? You can order any of the titles on the back of the books from our Mr. Men order line on 0870 787 1724. Orders should be delivered between 5 and 7 working days.

— TO BE COMPLETED BY AN ADULT —

To apply for any of these great offers, ask an adult to complete the details below and send this whole page with the appropriate payment and tokens, to: MR. MEN CLASSIC OFFER, PO BOX 715, HORSHAM RH12 5WG

☐ Please send me a giant-sized double-sided collectors' poster.
AND ☐ I enclose 6 tokens and have taped a £1 coin to the other side of this page.

☐ Please send me ☐ Mr. Men Library case(s) and/or ☐ Little Miss library case(s) at £5.99 each inc P&P

☐ I enclose a cheque/postal order payable to Egmont UK Limited for £...................

OR ☐ Please debit my MasterCard / Visa / Maestro / Delta account (delete as appropriate) for £...................

Card no. ☐☐☐☐ ☐☐☐☐ ☐☐☐☐ ☐☐☐☐ ☐☐☐☐ ☐☐☐☐   Security code ☐☐☐

Issue no. (if available) ☐   Start Date ☐☐/☐☐/☐☐   Expiry Date ☐☐/☐☐/☐☐

Fan's name: ....   Date of birth: ....

Address: ....

....

....   Postcode: ....

Name of parent / guardian: ....

Email for parent / guardian: ....

Signature of parent / guardian: ....

Please allow 28 days for delivery. Offer is only available while stocks last. We reserve the right to change the terms of this offer at any time and we offer a 14 day money back guarantee. This does not affect your statutory rights. Offers apply to UK only.

☐ We may occasionally wish to send you information about other Egmont children's books.
If you would rather we didn't, please tick this box.   **Ref: MRM 001**